The Adventures of Franklin

Beverly Bennett

WestBow Press books may be ordered through booksellers or by contacting:

WestBow Press
A Division of Thomas Nelson & Zondervan
1663 Liberty Drive
Bloomington, IN 47403
www.westbowpress.com
1 (866) 928-1240

Interior Image Credit: Kylee Childers

All Scripture quotations are taken from the King James Version.

ISBN: 978-1-9736-6900-5 (sc)
ISBN: 978-1-9736-6901-2 (e)

Library of Congress Control Number: 2019909435

Print information available on the last page.

WestBow Press rev. date: 08/16/2019

WESTBOW
PRESS®
A DIVISION OF THOMAS NELSON
& ZONDERVAN

This is a children's story of a popular firefly that lives in the hills of Missouri. His family must move to Alaska because of his father's job. There are no fireflies in Alaska. The town people stare at them and point fingers some even laugh. He is ashamed now because his family is different. Franklin meets a couple of mosquitos and a stinkbug that are trouble makers. They delight in bullying some of the town folk. The leader tells Franklin he can hang out with them if he hides his light. He agrees and begins to take part in things he knows is not right. Franklin watches as his new friends torment a Librarian (a book worm) and a Sunday school teacher (a praying mantis). Franklin has a dream that shakes him, and he turns his life around and once again becomes proud of who he is and even wins the stinkbug to the Lord.

My name is Beverly Bennett (Weber) I grew up in Marshall, Mo., the last of nine children. I moved to McDonald County Mo., when I was 23 and have lived there until the present. I have two children and five grandchildren. I was not raised in church. I got in church when my daughter was 9 months old, thanks to a sister in the Lord that let her light shine in front of me. I have been in church for 36 years and a Sunday school teacher almost as long. I am a member of LifePoint Pentecostal Church in Joplin, Mo., pastored by Fred Oates.

The illustrator is my granddaughter Kylee Childers. She is 13 years old and has been raised in church. She loves the Lord and loves to read.

I'm Franklin, one of the most popular fireflies in Stone County, Missouri. I have two best friends Sam and Oliver. We are best known for keeping our lights shining bright and flying fast. Every night the village children come out with mason jars in hand ready to see if this will be the night they catch us. Lucy, my little sister, loves to come watch us zip in and out among the children, squealing with pride each time we avoid the hands that would make us captives if we are a second to slow. Momma would ground Lucy and I both if she knew what we were up to on those warm summer evenings. Leo my older brother, rarely goes out. He is content in his room studying his Bible, listening to music or talking online to his friends all over the country.

One evening in June, Sam and I were sitting on the porch waiting for Oliver, so we could go on our evening mission. Lucy was playing in the yard waiting patiently.

"Look!" yelled Lucy. "Here comes Granny Dot!" Granny Dot was a widow woman who everyone loved. She had no children of her own, so she claimed all the neighborhood children as her grandbabies. She would often tell stories of her youth. She would close her eyes and say, "Oh I had the most vibrant red coat, accented with black spots in the perfect order across my back.

My how fast I could fly, in my younger days!" She was also known for the cookies she made. She won every year in the cookie contest at the county fair. She was carrying a tray of those delicious smelling cookies up the sidewalk, which Lucy gladly retrieved from her. Sam flew over to help Granny up the stairs. As I was getting up, I heard my mom and dad talking through the open screen door. I heard my mother say,

"Is there anything we can do about it?" Something in my mother's voice caught my attention.

"No, I'm afraid not. We have to go; we don't have a choice this time," my Father replied. Suddenly I was all ears.

"Oh Pete, the kids will be devastated! We have lived here their whole lives," said my mother.

"I know, we have been very fortunate, but it won't be forever. We will be able to move back in a couple of years. We knew it could come to this when I took this job, and I've heard Alaska is beautiful this time of year." I couldn't believe what I was hearing.

"Hello Franklin! What's wrong? You look like you have seen a lizard," said Granny Dot, chuckling.

"Worse, I just heard my dad tell my mom we are moving to Alaska," I replied as my heart began to beat faster.

"Oh, my goodness, well let's not panic," said Granny Dot, "your mom and dad know what's best for this family, and God is always in control. They will explain everything when the time is right."

That time came that very evening after dinner. Dad called us all together and told us his job was temporarily relocating us. We would be moving in one month. The next couple of weeks were a blur, packing, getting ready for the big move. Mom tried to make it easier. "It won't be so bad. It's only temporary, we will be back before you know it. Granny Dot will live in our house until we get back. She said you could come and spend a couple of weeks with her next summer. Your friends can come spend a couple of weeks with us too."

I tried everything to get my parents to change their mind. I said, "There are no lightning bugs in Alaska our family will be a bunch of outcasts." I even tried to convince them, dad could go alone to work in Alaska. Leo could assume the role of man of the house until he returned.

Nothing worked, and before I knew it, the mover came and loaded our stuff and we were headed down the road, the road to nothing.

"Look, Franklin! Isn't it pretty?" said Lucy

"Shut up Lucy, you have been talking ever since we got on the road." Coming from me those were harsh words to my little sister. She adored her big brother, but I didn't care. I was mad at the world.

"Franklin, there won't be any more of that kind of talk. Do you hear me?" said my dad. "You are not the only one that is having to move; it is not going to be easy for any of us. In fact, it will be a huge adjustment for everyone. We are going to bind together as a family and get through this. We will start by you apologizing to your sister."

Lucy's big brown eyes filling with tears gripped my heart for a second, I felt terrible. I apologized as I was told, and all was forgiven on Lucy's part. The scenery in Alaska was beautiful, and had I not been so angry, I would have enjoyed myself completely. There were huge mountains in the distance, a lot of trees, and lakes. The sunset was amazing with all the many colors against the brilliant blue sky. If only my best friends were here!

We would have the time of our lives. We would be spectacular lighting up the skies for those who had never seen a firefly.

Dad began to slow down a bit. We turned and headed up a long lane. Suddenly the trees parted, and there was a cottage made of stone, two stories with a front porch wrapped all the way around it. In the distance, I could see a pretty lake, the water sparkling silver in the evening light. Now being cooped up for so long, dad thought it would be a good idea for us to stretch our wings a bit. He said, "Let's fly into the village and see what it's like." It was just beginning to get dark, so all five of us flying together- lights blinking off and on – was drawing quite a bit of attention from the locals. I overheard a funny-looking dragon fly say,

"What in the world are those?" Another one said,

"I don't have a clue, maybe a government experiment?"

"Flying flashlights?" said another.

Some kids playing in the park started laughing and pointing at us, making fun of our tails blinking off and on. Dad flew down and circled them a few times. A little girl squealed with delight and tried to catch him. A group of rough- looking characters were leaned up against the slide pointing and laughing. If this was what school was going to be like, I was not looking forward to it.

My mom was very polite as usual, smiling and waving at everyone. Lucy was doing the same. Leo was just being Leo, just flying along. Taking it all in stride. I on the other hand was mortified. My face I'm sure was as bright as my tail I was so embarrassed, and for the first time in my life I was ashamed of my family and what we were. I tried hard not to blink my light. Perhaps no one would notice me if I kept my light off. We flew up and down the street a few times then headed home. I went straight to my room, miserable, and lonely. In a matter of days, I went from being the most popular firefly in the county to a misfit, a weirdo. Dad came to my room after a little while and said we needed to have a family discussion. We all gathered out on the porch. Dad began speaking, "I will say my peace; then everyone else will have a chance to talk. Now we all know that the folks around here don't know who we are or for that matter what we are. But folks will get used to us. Most people stare at those who may look or act different than what they are used to. We must give people a chance to get to know us. The only way to do that is to let our light shine so others will see our good works as the Lord shines through us. Soon folks will get to know us and will learn to love us, just like in our home town."

Tears of frustration welling up in my eyes. I said,

"But dad, they were laughing and.."

"Hold on let me finish," said Dad. "God made us the way we are. We didn't have a choice in that. But we do have a choice in our actions. We must hold our heads up and be proud of who we are. Others can't fault us for what we are, but they can fault us for how we act, and who we become. A lot of times people make fun of those they don't understand, and sometimes they even make fun of ones they are curious about or wish they were like. But once they see that making fun of you does not affect who you are or how you act, they usually come around and sometimes even become good friends. Now does anyone else have anything they would like to say?"

"Yes" said Leo "I'm not ashamed of being a firefly." I don't care if they laugh at me. It doesn't change who I am. We are a little funny after all" he said as he chuckled to himself. "Can I be excused? I want to read a little before I go online to catch up with my friends."

I seemed to be the only one this move effected. Days turned into weeks. Still I had not made any friends. I was sad, angry, lonely, and depressed. No one understood what I was going through.

Every time I would venture into town, it seemed like all eyes were on me. I went straight to school and straight home. We lived just outside of town, and there was no one I had anything in common with. One day when I was sitting under a tree down by the lake feeling sorry for myself. I heard voices coming from over the embankment. I inched my way up and peeked through the bushes. There were three fellas down by the water. The the two mosquitos I saw the first day we were in town, rough-looking, tough-talking guys. The other one was a bright purple stink bug. I didn't want them to see me, so I started inching my way backwards. Suddenly they were airborne flying right above me.

"Hey, who's that spying on us man?" said the stink bug. Before I knew it, they were on the bank beside me. "It's one of those weirdoes with the light-up body. What did they call them? Flying flashlights"? said one of the mosquitos. All three began to laugh. Weeks of built up anger came to the surface. I put my fist in the air and headed for the stink bug the biggest of the three. He stepped back a little startled by my reaction. I could smell him before I got close to him. Which slowed me down for a minute.

"Hold on buddy! "said the mosquito that seemed to be in charge. We are just having a little fun; we don't want any problems. We have never seen anyone like you before. My name's David; they call me Ace this here is John; we call him Swarm. The big guy over there is Earl; we call him Nose Plug for reasons you can guess." With that the two mosquitos laughed at him. "What's your name?" Ace continued. I let my hands down a little still watching the three close. "My name is Franklin; I'm a firefly from Missouri."

"Ok, Franklin from Missouri, you can hang with us if you want. Maybe we can fit you with a tail cover, so no one can see you glowing." They all laughed, and I turned red.

Nose Plug said, "I have an idea, let's put some mud on his tail. When it dries, you won't be able to see his light."

Now that was the best idea I heard since coming to Alaska. We all flew down by the lake. I scooted around in the mud until my light was completely covered. The two mosquitos flew beside me and lifted me off the ground. "Ok we will hold you in the air until the mud is dry." Said Swarm.

After about 20 minutes, I let my light shine and sure enough, you couldn't see it. Ace said,

"Alright, that's better, we will call you Ditch. Let's fly into town."

I thought to myself I had misjudged these guys. This is going to be great. I finally have some friends I can fly around with. For once I was excited to go into town.

As we came into town, Ace said

"Look! There is Miss Maggie, she is the Librarian. Let's go."

The three headed towards her, Ace first, them Swarm. Nose Plug was just ahead of me. I couldn't fly as fast because of the mud on my light. Swarm landed on her shoulder just as Ace landed on her forehead, Nose Plug began to circle her. She screamed and began to jump up and down trying to get them away from her. I could smell Nose Plug from where I had stopped. I had a clear understanding how he got his nickname. Ace bit her square on the nose and flew off. Immediately a red welt began to form. Swarm bit her twice and flew away, two more red welts formed. They were laughing and having a blast. "Come on, Ditch, get her." yelled Swarm. Looking at the welts on her and the cloud of stink around her, I really didn't want to do anything. I couldn't let my new friends down, so I flew into her hair. She was panicking now.

The library door opened, and an older man came out.

"Come on, it's Fred, let's go." said Ace and away they flew. I was a little bit behind and barely missed being caught.

They were laughing so hard and mimicking how Miss Maggie looked and acted. I felt bad for her. Next, we flew down the street to the church. Out under the tree was an elderly lady that appeared to be praying. Ace said, "This is old lady Miller. She has taught Sunday school since the beginning of time. Come on guys! Let's go."

In single file, they flew down. Ace and Swarm landed on her arms; she couldn't reach them to get them off. They bit her twice, I saw the red welts appear. They bit her again; a couple more welts popped up. Nose Plug landed on her glasses, knocking them to the ground as he let the stink go. I saw the cloud appear around her face and the tears come to her eyes. She began to cough and wave her hands in front of her face.

"You boys better stop! I'm going to call the Sheriff." They flew off in a flash. She looked at me with big eyes as she was feeling around for her glasses and said, "These boys are not good for you to be around; they will lead you into trouble. I flew down, picked up her glasses, and handed them to her our eyes locking for an instant. I thought of Granny Dot back home. I felt terrible for what they had done, but I flew off to join my new friends.

We headed out of town, back to the lake. I thought of the nights flying with my buddies back home. We never hurt anyone. My conscience was getting to me. I had made three friends, but this was not fun. We stayed by the lake for a little while. I washed the mud off my light, and headed home. The others took off for town.

This became the routine for us. We would meet at the lake hide my light in mud, fly into town torment whoever we could find, then fly back to the lake wash off my light, and head home. It got a little easier, but each time I would feel guilty and think to myself maybe I won't go with them tomorrow. Nose Plug began to come to the lake earlier than Ace and Swarm, we would skip rocks or lay on our backs picking animals out of the clouds, he would listen to me tell stories of back home while we waited for them to get there.

A couple of times we tried to get them to do something different, but they thought our suggestions were stupid.

One evening I came in just as mom was putting supper on the table. She said, "Well there you are! Supper is ready; you better get washed up." We all gathered around the table, Dad said the blessing asking that the Lord bless our food and our family and to always let us be a light to a world full of darkness. He thanked the Lord for providing for us and keeping us safe.

I felt guilty for the things I had been doing, but I told myself I really hadn't done anything wrong. I even helped some of the ones the others had tormented, like the Sunday School teacher. We finished eating, and mom and Lucy started clearing the table. I hadn't even spoken to Lucy today except to yell at her twice and tell her to get out of the way. I never talked to her like that back home. She was never this annoying back home, I don't think anyone realized how much the move had changed her.

Or so I told myself.

Just like every other evening dad got down the Bible we all gathered around, tonight he began reading Galatians 5:22-23. "But the fruit of the Spirit is love, joy, peace, longsuffering, gentleness, goodness, faith, meekness, temperance; against such the is no law. I tried to tune him out.

I knew God wasn't pleased with the things I had been involved in, but then I wasn't pleased with him making us move up here and leaving my friends.

"Alright everyone time to say our prayers and get to bed. We have church in the morning and Mrs. Miller has asked us to join her for lunch afterwards. I felt my heart drop to my knees. I had been avoiding her at church. I began to reason with myself. I'm sure she didn't recognize me; after all; my light was covered.

I never spoke to her. Surely if she had known it was me all along she would have told my dad by now. With these thoughts in mind, I headed to bed.

As I drifted off to sleep, I could see the hills of Missouri. There was Oliver and Sam sitting on the porch waiting for me, ready to go on our nightly mission. Where in the world was Lucy? She would never be late for the show. Something wasn't right with Sam and Oliver. I couldn't figure out what it was, they looked different. Maybe they had grown while I was gone? But that wasn't it. Wait a minute; both of their lights were out. As I got closer I could see their lights were covered with mud. There were other fireflies there too, and all their lights had mud on them. Granny Dot was sitting on the porch praying for protection for someone. I could hear my mom crying in the house.

I flew through the door and saw my mom and dad standing in the kitchen. I heard him say, "Stay strong Betsy. We will find her safe I promise."

Find her? Who was he talking about? "Dad, what's going on? Who is missing?" I said, but it was like my dad couldn't hear me. I saw my brother come in with several of the neighbors. He said," We can't look anymore tonight. We can't see anything in the woods; it's just to dark.

Our neighbor Ethel went over to my mom, as she put her arms around her she said, "Don't worry Betsy, the Lord will take care of Lucy; we will find her." My mind was running crazy. Lucy is missing in the woods; it is so dark in there.

No one has a visible light. Why don't they clean their lights off? We are fireflies; together we have enough lights to light up the entire forest. I spun around to check my light; it was covered in mud too. If only I could get this mud off my light, I could go save Lucy. I flew over to the sink and tried to wash it off. There was Ace, Swarm and Nose Plug. I said, "hey guys, help me get this mud off me. My little sister is lost in the forest. I need my light to be able to find her." Ace and Swarm began to laugh at me calling me a misfit and a weirdo. I said, "You can say whatever you want to about me, but the Lord made me just the way I am!" I saw the mud fall off my dad's light. "I'm proud to be a firefly!" His light was getting brighter each time I spoke. I said, "thank you Lord for giving me a light to shine in the darkness." Suddenly the mud started falling off everyone's light. The more I prayed and thanked the Lord the brighter their lights got. The room was a total glow. Dad yelled, "Come on guys! We have enough light to find her now." Off they went. My mom started praising the Lord with everything she had.

Ace, Swarm and Nose Plug disappeared. I could hear my dad and all the neighbors coming back. My dad yelled,"

We've found her she's ok, Betsy come quick!" My mom was flying through the door. I stood there watching everyone around me truly thankful we were a family of fireflies. I could hear my mom saying, "Where is Franklin?"

Dad hollered, "Franklin! You need to get up and get around we don't want to be late for church."

I came fully awake. Oh, my goodness it was only a dream. "Thank you, Lord for my family and our lights. Help me always to be proud of who I am. Forgive me Lord for the things I have done the past few weeks." I flew out of bed down the hall to see my little sister.

I said, "there you are, pretty as a picture."

Lucy looked surprised but threw her arms around me and said, "Momma said you would come around if we prayed for you and gave you a little time."

As we headed to church, I knew I had some apologizing to do to several people beginning with my family. I told them how sorry I was for acting the way I had and for the things I had been doing. I could tell this made my mom a little sad, but very happy.

Dad said all was forgiven and we would make things right and start over. As we flew into town, I saw Ace, Swarm and Nose Plug by the slide.

I said, "Mom, Dad you guys go ahead. I will catch up with you."

I flew down to them and told them I wouldn't be going with them anymore. I was sorry for not letting my light shine for everyone to see. Ace and Swarm started laughing. Nose Plug looked sad. I said, "We are on our way to church, and I want to invite all of you to join us." Ace and Swarm said, "No way!"

Nose Plug, looking at the ground said, "I think I might like to go." I said, "Great! Come on. It will be fun."

Ace said, "Are you kidding me, Nose Plug? No one wants you around them. The way you smell, they are going to laugh you right out of church, and when they do don't think you are going to come back to us." Swarm started laughing. I could see Nose Plug hesitate. I said, "No on will care, I promise. After church we can hang out together and do stuff that's really fun." He joined me, and we flew off together to catch up with my family. When we arrived at the church, Mrs. Miller was greeting at the front door.

I flew up to her and said, "Mrs. Miller I know you don't recognize me, but I need to apologize to you for my behavior over the past few weeks." She said, "I know who you are. I want you to know I have been praying for you from the very first time I saw you with the other three boys." Nose Plugs face turned red as she looked at him. Her eyes sparkled as she continued. "I forgive you." She turned to Nose Plug and welcomed him and asked him his name.

He said, "My name is Earl, I'm really sorry too."

She smiled at him and said, "I forgive you as well." I felt the guilt and burden of the past few weeks lift off my shoulders. I was truly happy for the first time since our move. As we took our seats I heard the Pastor say, "If we can turn our Bibles to Matthew chapter five."

He began to read verse 13.

"Ye are the salt of the earth: but if the salt have lost his savour, wherewith shall it be salted? It is thenceforth good for nothing, but to be cast out, and to be trodden under foot of men. (Matthew 5:13) Ye are the light of the world. A city that is set on a hill cannot be hid. (Matthew 5:14) I looked at my sister sitting with a small group of friends she had made and the rest of my family sitting on the pew beside us, and once again I thanked the Lord for my family and my new friend Earl.

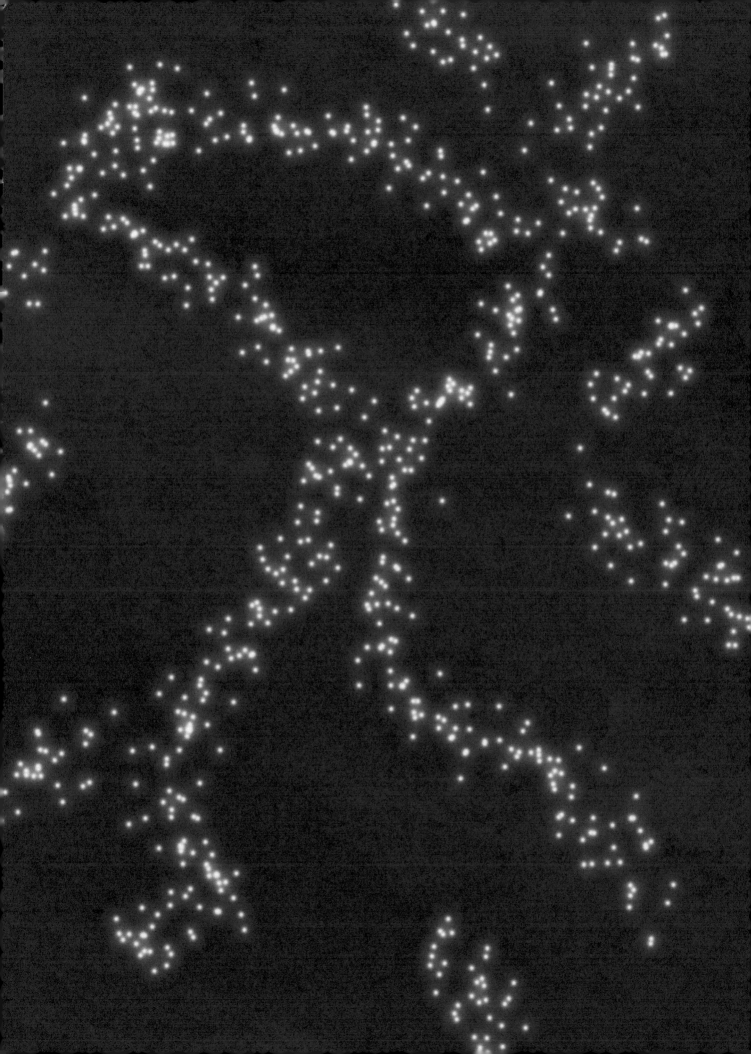